25.12.82

Dearest Simon,
A Happy Christmas
much love
Gaby + Mark

PENGUIN BOOKS
THE SITUATION IS HOPELESS

GW00750829

Ronald Searle was born in Cambridge in 1920. He studied art there before serving seven years in the army — half of them as a prisoner-of-war of the Japanese. After his release in 1945, he began free-lancing from London and was soon contributing to publications all over the world. Ronald Searle has published some fifty books, either alone or in collaboration. Since 1961 he has lived in France. Penguin also publish his book *The Square Egg*. This book was originally published under the title *The King of Beasts and Other Creatures* (Allen Lane 1980).

The Situation is Hopeless

RONALD SEARLE

The Situation is Hopeless

PENGUIN BOOKS

Penguin Books Ltd, Harmondsworth, Middlesex, England
Penguin Books, 625 Madison Avenue, New York, New York 10022, U.S.A.
Penguin Books Australia Ltd, Ringwood, Victoria, Australia
Penguin Books Canada Ltd, 2801 John Street, Markham, Ontario, Canada L3R 1B4
Penguin Books (N.Z.) Ltd, 182-190 Wairau Road, Auckland 10, New Zealand

First published in Great Britain
as *The King of Beasts and Other Creatures*
by Allen Lane 1980
First published in the United States of America
by The Viking Press (A Studio Book) 1981
Published in Penguin Books 1982

Copyright © Ronald Searle, 1980
All rights reserved

Made and printed in Great Britain by
William Clowes (Beccles) Limited
Beccles and London

Except in the United States of America,
this book is sold subject to the condition
that it shall not, by way of trade or otherwise,
be lent, re-sold, hired out, or otherwise circulated
without the publisher's prior consent in any form of
binding or cover other than that in which it is
published and without a similar condition
including this condition being imposed
on the subsequent purchaser

Exhibitionist donkey
about to make an ass of itself

Fastidious rat looking for an
impeccable sewer

Hypersensitive rattlesnake
in search of peace and quiet

Cretinous owl utterly convinced
that it is revered as a symbol of wisdom

Particularly repellent dog glowing
under the impression that it is man's
best friend

Imbecile rodent confident that
it has a foolproof claim against the
Disney Organization

Loquacious parrot convinced
that it is teaching man a basic vocabulary

Obtuse camel looking for a largish needle

Out-of-touch unicorn unaware that it is a myth

Agnostic serpent attempting to sell apples

Baby seal under the impression
that clubs are centres of social activity

Exceptionally obese hippopotamus
trying to reassure itself that Fat is Fun

Retarded ape happy in the
knowledge that it is the ancestor of Man

American bald eagle suddenly realizing that
its leanings are basically Marxist

Misinformed crocodile shedding genuine tears

Feeble-minded circus lion basking
in the belief that it is the King of Beasts

Hypochondriac cow going for a cholesterol test

Simple-minded wart-hog reassuring itself
that beauty is more than skin deep

Naïve asp seeking a bosom friend

Hopelessly mixed-up vampire bat
trying to conceal the fact that its tastes
are rigidly vegetarian

Asinine horse thinking that
it is only a question of time before it
replaces the car

Under-sexed double-horned rhinoceros
in search of a reliable aphrodisiac

Muddled sheep in wolf's clothing

Aggressive chicken applying Kung Fu
to a Peking Duck

Conceited egg about to commence its memoirs

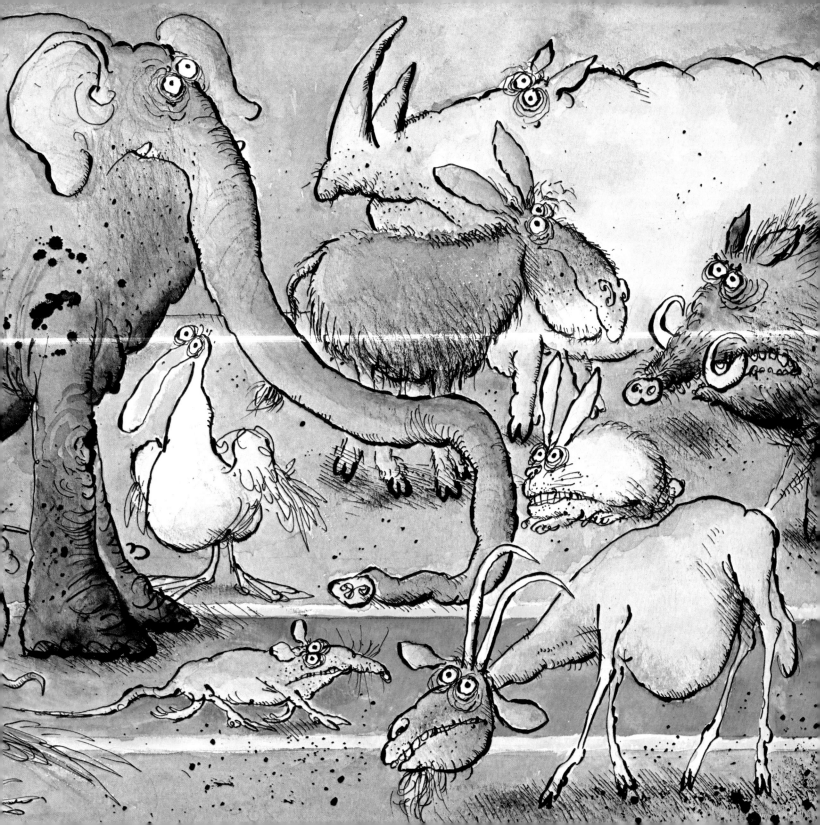